That Night (Was Enough To...)

Cyscoprime Publishers

An Imprint of Evincepub Publishing

Parijat Extension, Bilaspur, Chhattisgarh 495001

First Published by Cyscoprime Publishers 2020

ISBN: 978-93-90047-19-2

Price: Rs.110/-

THAT Night (was enough to….)

By

Aditya Sharma

About The Book

This is an amazing story of an eleven-year-old girl. It deals with the chaos of night which brought drastic change in the life of a sweet little girl to which she is unknown. It is a short and crisp story has essence of what next in it...

The detailing of scenes and characters make this book alive and interesting for the readers.

About The Author

Aditya Sharma is a 22 years old boy. Who is a medical student and pursuing MBBS.

This is his first ever short novel, though he is going to be a doctor but his passion of writing made him to write this short novel...

He is a voracious reader and loves his other work that he has done till now like he has written several poems –

Yaad si aagyi....
Nanhi si jaan......
Waqt, zindagi and khamoshi......

After his graduation also he wants to continue his writing.

ACKNOWLEDGEMENTS

Once again, I am faced with the task of showing gratitude to people who helped me while I was working on this short novel, more than anything, I am grateful to each one of them, for constantly supporting me, never give up on me.

I thank my entire family for dealing with whatever I put them through—but especially I want to thank my Maa-Papa, as u already know – you are the best parents, much love.

Shivangi Bhadana -- Thank you, for inspiring me to write my first ever short novel.... And see I finally did it...

Toyesha Raman – I really want to thank you for editing my work... and suggesting valuable inputs for its improvement. I really mean that your words made it look better.

Aditi Sharma – thank you for reading it just when I completed the writing and gave suggestions about it and thanks for much appreciation.

And a very big thank to each and every reader ... I am eternally grateful ......

Table of Contents

THAT NIGHT

(WAS ENOUGH TO…...)

Usually nights are more beautiful than days- the moment the sun sets, people find themselves more enthusiastic to begin the life they actually want to live.

The moon shines and the stars twinkle while the blanket of darkness wraps the world but it is priceless for those who lost their ability to dream due to the encroaching rays of sun, which shatters them throughout.

"I love the silent hour of night, for blissful dreams may then arise,
Revealing to my charmed sight what may not bless my waking eyes,"

--- Anne Bronte.

These lines amazingly capture the ethos of night, and tells how the silence and peace are merged in the heart of night, and the most fascinating thing is that the night comes with dreams that may take someone to the virtual world, totally different.

Eyes are blessed, as they have charmed sight that can rejuvenate the feeling even in the beautiful darkness of night. The more the darkness, the brighter the stars are...

Life is not only how we live in the presence of the rays but it is also the mystery that the night possesses.

Night also has many secrets embedded in the darkness too.

Though the night is beautiful but at the same time it may be dangerous for some as an uncanny fear does grip us all

This story is going to deal with the darkness of night and the pressing question- is it awful or full of bliss?

Chapter 1

It is the time when the huge bells of kali mandir start ringing with the *Nagadas,* in the town called Durgapur in West Bengal. Every day, this means it's the time to worship Goddess *Kali.*

It was around 7'o clock in the evening when the priest of Kali Mandir began with blowing conch and lit the lamp. The enthralling sound of conch reaches the girl who is sitting beside the river on the wet stairs of the holy bath with her feet in the water. The sky was pink with blue rays as the sun was about to set, it seems like an orange has fallen from the tree and is going to get drowned in the river soon.

The cold breeze coming from river swishes her hair which gets entangled, so she tries to tie them up but it is not possible for her as her silky hair loses the knot when the breeze swishes past her hair again.

She is an eleven-year-old with dark eyes and brown skin. The moment she hears the sound of conch and bells she lifts her head with a smile, trying to remember what she forgot. Yes! she had to worship goddess Kali this evening.

She takes her legs out of the water and runs towards the temple. She doesn't say anything to her younger brother *Gunnu,* a nine-year-old playing with his friends nearby.

When he sees that his sister is going away and he tries to run after her saying *"Munmun kothaiye jacchi."*

She was in a haste so she didn't hear him. She wanted to reach the temple as soon as possible to attend the Sandhya aarti of Mahakali. Munmun took a short cut to reach the temple but in that haste, she forgot to wear her slippers, she was bare foot and running over the grass, so her feet were marred with dust but she didn't care.

Gunnu instead of chasing her, ran towards his house where his mother *Polomi,* was cooking food for the night.

Polomi lived in a hut with her two children and her husband *Deboshish.* Deboshish was not at home. Gunnu comes all of a sudden and tells her that her daughter ran away without telling him where she went.

Polomi started to worry, she left the uncut vegetables on the floor and came out of the hut looking for Munmun. Owing to the poverty, she didn't have money to buy herself a proper saree with a blouse, so she went out of the house wearing a 6yard long red cloth she considered a saree despite the fact that it was torn from below.

Polomi started calling out her daughter's name loudly –

"Munmun! Munmun!"

Chapter 2

Aarti was about to finish, but Munmun was still on her way. She was running to reach, she started sweating and breathing heavily and suddenly, her ankle twisted but this didn't stop her, she started limping a bit but the zeal in her heart made her to run much faster, this shows the devotion she had towards the Goddess, the stunning view of the evening had distracted her before but now all she wants is to attend the aarti .

The moment she was about to reach, by the corner of her eyes she saw a squirrel. Munmun didn't go any further, she could feel her heart beating but she had no idea why she stopped.

But she didn't question herself, even though for the first time in her life, she was not going to attend the aarti, her heart didn't allow her to go away because the squirrel was taking its last breaths.

It was lying down on its back over the clay with its belly facing the sky. Its mouth was open, gasping for breath but it seemed as if the squirrel wanted to say something, it's leg was bleeding immensely and neck was badly injured. It seems that something attacked at it but it managed to escape somehow, but not enough to fight for its life for long, it's open mouth and widened eyes showed the dread of that realization in it's face.

Munmun's heart completely melted when she saw the terrifying condition of the squirrel on the verge of death. She quickly scrammed towards the squirrel and just by seeing her in such an awful situation, tears started to flow, she immediately picked it softly and put it on her lap, her hands were shaking and she got numb but also furious on herself that she couldn't able to help it out, the only thing which stuck in her mind was how can she save it's life, at this moment the aarti of Goddess got over as the last bell rang and sound of conch and Nagadas stopped coming.

With that note Munmun realized, that this evening she missed the worship, Munmun felt the guilt about it but now her main aim was to save the squirrel's life. So she took it and got up and started running towards her friend *Champa's* house, because Champa's father has some knowledge of ayurveda, so she thought he might save her.

But after a moment, she realized that the squirrel was no more, its neck was hanging down in her hand. She started screaming, crying and accusing herself for its death.

While doing so she sat on her knees and kissed the squirrel goodbye. Her throat was choking while crying, she got hiccups and it seemed as if she had lost someone very special but it actually was a little soul with whom she had met a few minutes back. She spent around half an hour with its lifeless body and then she decided to bury it in the heart of earth. So quickly she completed the journey towards kali mandir, and went at the back of the temple. She thought of burying it behind the temple because she thinks that Maa kali will take its soul in her protection. She dug the earth with a broken wooden stick, she was trying hard to dig properly but her soft, little, tiny hands managed to dig a shallow grave but it was sufficient enough for the little body to rest in peace.

While still having tears in her eyes she buried the little squirrel. Through it all, she forgot about the pain in her twisted ankle, but now that she started walking towards her home, she felt the pain again and started limping.

It was around 7:48 and the darkness of night engulfed the pink sky slowly, Munmun still feeling the grief in her heart, she bowed her head in front of the idol of the Goddess asking for forgiveness as she didn't attend the aarti and ended the apology by saying- "I left a tiny soul in your protection Maa".

On the other hand, Polomi was really concerned for her daughter, she had never been so late before, her motherly instincts made her overthink- has

something happened to her? It got her even more anxious to know about Munmun's whereabouts.
Gunnu couldn't care much. He started playing with the twigs which were lying beside the block of mud which they used to put their torn clothes on. Playing with those twigs while lifting them in air somehow made him happy.
But Polomi started hyperventilating. She wasn't able to find Munmun on her own so she waited for Deboshish to come to help her find their daughter, she was feeling utterly helpless.
She started praying to the Goddess, in a hope that she will protect her, where ever she is.

Chapter 3

It was around 8:00pm, the blanket of darkness had taken over the sky, the temperature started decreasing, the wind blew faster than before. Large black clouds spread all over the sky making Polomi feel gloomy. It was about to drizzle which made Polomi more desperate to find her daughter.

After a while, Polomi spots her daughter, she ran and hugged her daughter tightly even before she could reach the house. Then she scolded her daughter and asked her where she was.

Munmun, still reeling from guilt didn't utter a word and stayed silent. This angered her mother even more, she asked again but before Munmun could answer, Polomi saw the blood stain on her skirt. She forgot her anger and became really worried. She snaps and asks about the stain, Munmun replied in a very low tone – "it's the stain of a dead squirrel". Then she narrated the whole incident, meanwhile it started drizzling, Polomi took her inside. Weather turned really cold.

(Instead of appearing mesmerizing, today this night brought nothing but darkness and a mysterious melancholic aura with itself)

The stars hid behind the clouds. The Moon tries to peep between the clouds and to further make the matters worse, the wind was howling outside.
Polomi somehow grasped the omen the night brought with itself.
She started cutting the vegetables which she left uncut. In her heart she was thanking the goddess to protect her but she still felt an unknown fear in her mind.
(Now this Night had something else to say, as it started raining heavily)
The water started dripping from the roof of hut which was made up of mud bricks. Polomi placed a parat (a utensil of widened mouth) under the spot to stop the water from falling on the floor.
Munmun changed her skirt and sat with Gunnu to have last meal of the day.
Now it was around 8:30, Deboshish came home with his clothes dipping wet, with him there were two more men.
Polomi smiled at her husband, he came home after working at the Thakur's Haveilly.
(Deboshish works as a servant in the Haveilly of Thakurs of that area, ***Thakur Suryabhan Chakraborty*** is like a king for the people of Durgapur. He is the zamindar of Durgapur.)
Polomi asked Deboshish about the two men that came with him, she had never seen them before.

Instead of answering about it, he gave her a big smile and showed her 10 gold coins.

Polomi immediately asked– "where did you get these coins from?"

Deboshish answered – "These coins were given by Thakur Suryabhan, and these two are Thakur's personal assistants who have come here to take Munmun with them to the haveilly."

Polomi couldn't believe what he said. Her eyes widened with shock, her face went pale and tears were threatening to flow, she started sweating after hearing this news, her lower jaw dropped, for a while she lost her consciousness, but managed to arrange herself as the assistants were present in the house.

"NO!" -the word came out of her mouth.

She completely denied. She said will never send her daughter to the haveilly. Deboshish grabbed her hand furiously and said "Don't forget the promise we made to Thakur Suryabhan when Munmun was born."

(Eleven years ago, when Munmun was born, Deboshish and polomi had nothing. They were jobless, begging for food. At that time, Thakur Suryabhan had offered him a job of servant in his haveilly but only on one condition- when their newborn crosses ten years of age, they have to send her to his haveily where she will work as a servant of Thakur's children.)

Having heard this, Polomi broke in tears, she didn't want her child to leave , but she couldn't do anything as they promised him.

This night had completely changed the life of Polomi, Deboshish and Munmun.

Munmun was waiting for dinner, unbeknownst to the storm that just hit her.

It was around 9'0 clock, Polomi dressed up Munmun, and saying that now you have to spend the rest of your life in haveilly, she didn't understand what her mother was trying to say.

Deboshish and Polomi had to send their daughter, Gunnu was with them.

Munmun (kept wailing and saying she doesn't want to go) sat in the chariot that was going towards the haveilly while the assisstants sat with her.

Polomi and Deboshish broke in tears, feeling helpless,

Polomi fell on the ground shouted loudly- "*Munmun!!*"

Chapter 4

The wooden chariot had windows made of glass, Munmun was inside it with two strangers who she had never seen before. She was scared so she didn't even look up, this little girl had a thought of fleeting away but couldn't try to do so.

She sat in the corner and put her right hand on the wooden rim of the chariot, she hid her face with the elbow of left hand, being short in height her feet were above the floor , the horses were running swiftly, the path was bumpy and through the jungle, the chariot was shaking so badly that Munmun wasn't able to balance herself and fell on floor of chariot, and small idol of Maa Kali fell from her hand (which was given by Polomi when she was leaving the home and told her to always keep this with herself) she immediately pick the statue and sat back again in the corner.

The assistant tried to talk to her and make her feel comfortable but she kept her mouth shut and didn't utter a single word.

With time, the fervor of night climbed, the weather cleared and it stopped raining, Munmun could see the stars through the window, and the full moon appeared and covered everything in its shiny, silver light.

However, the moon appeared to red, it depicted that something erroneous was going to happen, but Munmun had no idea about it. The assistant offered her some berries to eat and though she was feeling hungry as she didn't have dinner, she refused to take them and sat in the corner.

It was around 9:45, they had to reach as early as possible (Thakur had ordered them that he wanted that girl in haveilly before 10 of this night) so they ordered the charioteer to ride even faster.

Dhamu hit the horses with the leather rope and pulled it backwards so that horses run much faster, Munmun was thinking about her parents and her younger brother Gunnu, she was crying inside her heart and sought solace in the statue she held by holding the Goddess as tightly as she could.

They had a long way to go. Munmun had nothing but one question about it- "What was she doing in the chariot?"

They were about to cross the river via a bridge. Suddenly, a gloomy light fell on her face, she lifted her head and tried to peep through the window, it was the reflection of moon light from the river water. The serenity of this reflection made her lips twitch into a smile.

It seemed that the night was unending. It felt as if the sun would never rise again.
This Night was enough for a life to come to an end.

Now the sky was clear, the stars were shinning, but shade of red moon tried to make an impact. This whole scenario defined the behavior of night.
It was around 10:20. They were about to reach. They started climbing on the highland as the haveilly was on top of a hill. Dhamu pulled the rope backwords and made the horses climb the highland effortlessly. He knew how to handle the horses in such circumstances.
Now Munmun was able to see a huge haveilly in which she is going to enter soon.
This haveily had its own royal grandeur, Munmun had never seen such a huge haveilly before, around 10:30 they entered in the haveilly through a huge wooden door of wood which is was carved and painted in several colours.
Dhamu parked the chariot in the porch which had several beautiful plants emitting pleasant fragrances. She could smell those. There were so many servants moving here and there, busy making some arrangements.
Munmun got out of the chariot with the idol in her hand. Everybody stopped working and stared at

Munmun as they all knew she was going to come in this haveilly.

(It has always been said that big places have their own secrets and this time it seemed right.)

The assistants brought her to the Thakur, who was lying on his bed and his wife Sulochana was making paan for him, but Sulochana had no idea why this little girl had arrived.

Suryabhan passed a smile and ordered the assistant to take her to the Sringar room and get her ready like a bride. On hearing this Munmun felt shocked as she was told that she had to live like a servant and had to serve Thakur's children, she screamed and cried and tried to run but the assistants held her tightly. They snatched the idol from her hand and took her to the sringaar room where they ordered the two maids to get Munmun ready like a beautiful bride.

Everyone who was present in the haveilly like servants, gardners, charioteers, assistants and many more, knew deep in their hearts all the secrets hiding behind the huge walls of haveilly.

The two maids took munmun inside the sringaar room and closed the door. Munmun was yelling, but no one appeared to hear her screams as if they ignored it because they couldn't help her.

Chapter 5

Sulochana was curious to know why Suryabhan wanted her to look bridal. She asked him about Munmun.

Suryabhan got irritated and lifted the end of his *Dhoti* by his left hand and simultaneously put a bright red turban on his head. He frowned and said, "Stay out of this." And left the room.

Sulochana felt there was something fishy, so just after he left, she ran towards DUSH MAHAL where her mother-in-law stayed. While crossing the gate of her room her sari got stuck in the gate so she pulled it and the end of her sari got torn, she picked that torn cloth and made a knot of it and fixed it at her waist.

She went to her mother-in- law and asked her about Munmun (As her mother-in-law was very close to Thakur, so Sulochana thought that she must know about her.)

Her mother-in-law's hair had completely turned grey, she was a wearing black sari. Feeling emotional about Munmun she started telling Sulochna everything. First she told her about the second wife of Suryabhan Thakur- *Shambhavi Das.*

Two years back, Shambhavi had met with an accident and went in comatose. Her brain worked but her body lay lifeless.

She was the most loved wife of Suryabhan. Thakur used to spend a lot of time with her. But after that incident, Thakur Suryabhan broke from inside, he did everything to get her back to her normal state but to no avail.

But 2 months back, he met with a prude named *Baba Shondas* who had knowledge how to use black magic. Thakur just wanted his wife back so he started meeting with that man.

Her mother in law stopped, she wiped her tears away. Sulochana got more curious to know that what Shondas had asked Thakur to do.

Sulochana sat near the bed and begged her to tell the truth, her mother in law told her, shaking and stammering, he said that there is only a way to get Shambhavi back to normal and for that, he has to sacrifice an eleven year old married girl in front of fire at midnight under the full moon in the sky.

Thakur had immediately accepted because all he wanted was his wife. So he thought about the daughter of Deboshish and

Polomi, who had already promised him to send their daughter. So he had ordered his assistants to bring Munmun in the haveilly. He will marry her first and then exactly at mid night under the redness of full moon he will sacrifice the little girl for his wife Shambhavi.

It was around 11 of the night, Sulochana understood the ruckus about to happen and wanted to stop this cruel deed but her mother in law stopped her and said she won't be able to save that little girl because Shondas and Thakur have already closed all the doors of haveilly, Sulochana immediately turned to see that the door of Dush mahal was also locked.

They both were helpless, feeling guilty in their hearts.

On the other hand, Munmun was dressed a white saari having broad bright red border. She had no clue what was going to happen with her in next few minutes. She tried hard to get rid of everything she wore but her weak body couldn't remove it. Soon she was brought at a place where no one was allowed to enter other than Munmun, Thakur Suryabhan and Shondas.

The room was completely dark. Shondas had made everything ready and started reciting some mantras which hypnotized the little girl. Now Munmun was under his control and she did everything she was asked to do.

This night with the red moon has changed everything for Munmun. A few hours back when she was running to attend the aarti of Mahakali, she had no idea what this night had in store for her.

This room was all dark all around, and had no roof, Munmun could see the stars but now she won't appreciate them,

Shondas made her sit beside the fire and Thakur sat next to her.

Shondas with a skull in one hand and bone in other started reciting mantras, Munmun was quiet and wasn't saying anything but continuously stared at the fire, her eyes turned red brimming with and her body turned pale but still she was under his control.

Soon they got married, now there was just 15 minutes left to midnight, although the sky was clear but suddenly lightning occurred with a thunderous sound, which clearly depicts the chaos of this night.

Munmun was a eleven year old married girl now only a scapegoat for them. Shondas and Suryabhan were ready for the human sacrifice.

Munmun had no idea what was happenin. Thakur made her lie down and brought a sharp sword. Shondas was reciting mantras continuously.

(This night has come with a drastic change in several lives, Polomi lost her daughter, Deboshish felt guitly, Gunnu had no sister to run behind.)

This night was enough to ruin the cloud of happiness.

It was midnight, the moon was clear in the sky and Thakur was with his sword in his hands, he was waiting for the signal of Shondas so that he can sacrifice her neck in the fire.

Thakur was sweating, the sword was slipping from his hand but he tried to grab it tightly, he lifted the sword up in the air with both the hands and was ready for the process.

The moment Shondas was finished with the mantras, he gave a signal to Thakur Suryabhan by lifting his left eyebrow and bending his neck down towards the right side, now Suryabhan got the signal and he swung his arms with all his might and aimed for the head of the little girl (with heavy tone)

Ahhhhhhhhhhh..........

I opened my eyes in shock. I was not fully conscious yet but I found myself lying on bed, I was sweating from head to toe. My body was shivering and all I thought about in this darkness of the night was Munmun. Initially I had no idea that what had happened but soon I realized it was all a nightmare. Now I was wide awake, I immediately looked at the clock and it was exactly midnight.

Somehow I composed myself and ran towards my daughter's room to look if is she fine or not? I reached her room and switched on the lights. She was sleeping quietly in her bed. My throbbing heart finally relaxed. I sat beside her and kissed her forehead.

(I must say...THAT NIGHT was enough to change the view of happiness. Whether it was for me or for Munmun...)

By

Aditya Sharma

www.ingramcontent.com/pod-product-compliance
Ingram Content Group UK Ltd.
Pitfield, Milton Keynes, MK11 3LW, UK
UKHW040014200726
13854UKWH00001B/192

9 789390 047192